You can't be friends

with a troll, Dotti!

To Rosie,

Happy reading!

Much love

Caroline

x

Caroline Meech

This story is entirely a work of fiction (although if you do know any trolls, please do let me know.). The names, characters and incidents portrayed in it are the work of the author's imagination. Any resemblance to actual persons, living or dead, events or localities is entirely coincidental.

1

If you believe you can, you will.

For the Meechlets many

And to all the children who have inspired me

with their love, acceptance and creativity.

This book is for you,

love from Mrs Meech.

X

Also to Mike, my biggest supporter.

X

A letter from the author...

I love writing stories. After I wrote my
first book for grown-ups my children
asked when I would write one for them.
So, here it is.

I spent five years working in schools
where one of my jobs was to help children
learn to love reading. Sometimes they
hadn't found the book that sparked that
joy, and sometimes they just found it
really hard to read the words properly.

My youngest daughter Alice is just like
this. She told me one day that it was
hard to read because the words wriggled
and swirled on the page. I set out to find
out why and soon we found out from two
lovely ladies, called Lisa and Gheeda, that
Alice has something called Visual Stress.

Alice now wears special glasses that have
coloured lenses and reading is much
easier for her. Alice also chose the font

that I've used in this book because she can read it more easily.

When thinking about the cover for this book I ran a competition at Crestwood Community School in Eastleigh to find a talented artist. The entries were all brilliant in their own way, each having its own creative flair. The winner, Luke Bird (age 13), was chosen because as soon as I saw his pictures I knew he'd captured the essence of Dotti and Terence perfectly! I've used his pictures as the basis for the drawings throughout the book.

I hope you enjoy reading this story, please tell me what you think of it, and what adventures you think Dotti will encounter next!

Caroline

Visit me at
www.carolinemeechauthor.com

Dotti loved her bed. The warm, cosy, snuggly feeling never failed to make her happy. Her dreams always seemed to be warm and fuzzy too and even when she knew it was morning, her mind registering the crack of light shining through the curtains, she still kept her eyes shut. Every morning had the same routine.

"Wake up, Dotti!" her mum sang cheerfully.

"Ugh," she groaned, her eyes still shut. "Don't want to."

"Come on, you must go to school."

"Ten more minutes?" Dotti begged, one eye open.

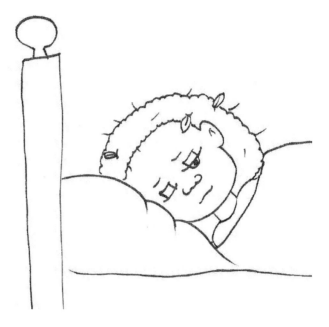

"I'm afraid not, Love. You'll be late if you don't get up now," her mum insisted.

"Then why don't you let me go across the bridge. It'll be *loads* quicker, *and* I could stay in bed longer!"

Dotti tried to persuade her.

Her mum answered impatiently, cross that Dotti asked the same thing every day. "You know why, Dotti. Don't keep on. I've told you before, it's dangerous. That smelly, ugly, hairy, grumpy old troll lives under the bridge and if you try to cross, he will eat you for breakfast."

Dotti and her parents lived in a picture-perfect cottage, you know the sort. It had white painted brick walls, a straw thatched roof, little wooden windows and roses growing around the front door. It had a beautiful garden, tended to lovingly by her Dad. In it stood fruit trees that were perfect for climbing, and it had a flawless green carpet of grass that led down to a babbling river. Across the river was the bottom end of the school field which could be accessed by an old wooden bridge. The perfect short cut to school! At least it would be if it weren't for the smelly, ugly, nose-picking, child-eating troll.

Dotti rolled her eyes, "Oh don't be silly Mum, he can't be *that* bad!"

"Do you want to be gobbled up on the way to school?" her mum asked crossly.

"Maybe he doesn't eat children. Maybe he's just grumpy because no-one talks to him," Dotti replied defiantly.

"Well, you're not going to find out, young lady. Up you get!" and she gave Dotti a look that said NOW!

At eight years old, Dotti was a force to be reckoned with. She knew exactly how she liked to wear her thick curly black hair; that her carrots should be raw and never cooked; that her cucumber should be cut into fingers and not rounds, and the difference between right and wrong. She also knew, however, that when something didn't feel right, she *had* to find out why.

She pulled back her bed covers, got up, and walked across to the bedroom window. Peering through the glass she could see the early morning steam rising from the river. Her Dad had always told her it was troll breath. *Poor old troll*, she thought to herself, *it can't be nice knowing that no-one likes you. You must be very lonely.*

Dotti wondered more about what she'd been told. *Don't worry Mr Troll. I won't let you be lonely anymore.* And with that she decided *she* would become the troll's first friend.

Dressed in her green summer playsuit and odd socks, Dotti bounded down the stairs for breakfast. She sat at the wooden kitchen table that had been marked over the years by milk, ketchup and felt-tip pens. Her mum put two slices of wholemeal bread on the plate in front of her spread thickly with marmite. Dotti's favourite.

Her mum danced to the radio as she packed Dotti's lunchbox while her Dad made cups of tea. Dotti ate one slice of toast and left the other untouched.

"Eat your breakfast up, Love," her mum said. "I don't want it wasted."

"It won't be wasted, Mum," Dotti answered earnestly. "I'm going to give it to the troll."

Her mum stopped what she was doing and turned to face her. "Why on earth would you do that?" she asked in a stern voice.

"Because I want to be his friend," Dotti replied, shrugging her shoulders.

Her mum laughed, shocked and amused at the same time. "You can't be friends with a troll, Dotti! Trolls don't want to be friends with people, they want to eat them!"

"Well I think you're wrong. I've never seen him eating people, have you?"

Her mum, struggling to reply, turned to her Dad for support. Her Dad shrugged.

Seizing her opportunity, Dotti picked up her plate and dashed out of the back door, her mum's calls of "Dotti!" trailing behind her.

As she reached the bottom of the garden, Dotti slowed, her heart thumping in her chest. She stepped tentatively towards the rickety old bridge. Gently, she tip-toed onto the first wooden step.

"Who's that stepping on MY bridge?" a voice roared. "I'll eat you up if you dare to cross!"

Shaking, she stammered "I, I,

thought you might be hungry," stumbling back, she dropped the plate on the grass and ran back up the garden towards the house as fast as she could.

As she floundered through the back door her mum, hands on hips, scolded "I told you he'd eat you up!"

"He didn't eat me," Dotti gasped, breathlessly. "He just *told* me he'd eat me, that's different."

Dotti stared out of the classroom window later that day, the troll occupying her thoughts. The more she considered what she'd been told about him, the more she thought it couldn't be true. After all, no children had ever been eaten as far as she could remember. Sure, it did sometimes smell a bit...eggy, at the bottom of the garden and she'd heard his ferocious voice for herself, but apart from that everything else seemed to be hearsay.

She'd never actually *seen* the troll so she couldn't say if he was ugly, and even if he was, it didn't matter to her. The more she thought about it, the more she knew that she had find out the truth.

3

That evening, Dotti was sat at the kitchen table doing her homework when the doorbell rang. She would normally call for her mum, who was upstairs, but for some reason curiosity took over and she ran to answer it.

When she opened the door, stood in a row were three men in overalls, each taller than the man to his left. The shortest man had black scruffy hair and buck teeth. The middle-sized man had brown scruffy hair, buck teeth and a brown goatee beard sprouting out of his long chin. The tallest, and oldest of the men, had grey scruffy hair, buck teeth, a grey goatee beard and was chewing on a long piece of liquorice which stuck out of the side of his mouth like a piece of straw.

"Hello?" questioned Dotti.

The men introduced themselves.

"Benji," nodded the shortest.

"Bobby," nodded the middle-sized man.

"Bill," finished the tallest.

The short man spoke again "Good afternoon, Missy, is yer Ma in?"

The middle man spoke next "Yeah, yer Ma called us. We got a job to do out back, ain't we Bill?"

Dotti frowned, unsure as to what

they wanted.

The older man spoke last, his voice much stronger and clearer to understand. "Yup." He chomped on his liquorice. "Afternoon Miss, your mum called us earlier today, said you had some, er, vermin you need sorting in the garden."

As he spoke, Bill handed Dotti his business card.

Dotti gasped. She needed to form a plan, and quickly, as she realised what they were here to do.

"Dotti! Who is it Love?" her mum called from upstairs. "I'll be down in just a moment."

"It's OK Mum, I've got it covered!" she shouted back. "Sorry," she said to the older man, noticing his grey overalls were covered in mud. "Mum's in the loo," she whispered behind her hand, "she could be *some time.*" Blushing slightly the men raised their abnormally hairy eyebrows. "Actually, I think you might be too late," she continued.

"Too late?" the tall man asked.

"Oh yes. Another man was here earlier bundling something smelly and hairy into the back of his van. Mum paid him some money and he left. I must say, I don't envy him having to drive with that stench behind his seat!" Dotti waved her hand in front of her nose, accentuating the whiff.

"Awwww, we're too late!" the youngest man whined. "An' I was lookin' forward to a good ol' troll roasting tonight," he looked disappointed and stamped his foot childishly before returning to their van.

"Are you sure, Miss?" the tall man asked suspiciously, still chomping.

"Yup!" replied Dotti, smiling her sweetest smile.

"Right you are then, if there's any more trouble, call us again," he gave Dotti a funny look before getting back into his van and driving off.

Breathing a sigh of relief, Dotti closed the front door. *Thank goodness for that!* She thought to herself. *I hope I've done the right thing! I think it's time I find out what this troll is really like...*

4

This time Dotti prepared properly for meeting a troll. She was armed with air freshener (to spray away the smelliness) and a clothes peg on her nose; sunglasses (to shield her from the ugliness), tissues (for any stray bogies) and a plate of cooked sausages left over from dinner to tempt him away from eating her. She'd also written a short note:

Dear Troll

Pleeze will you be my frend?

Love Dotti

P.S. I dont tayste very nice xxx

Taking a deep breath, she opened the back door to a pleasant surprise. There on the step was the plate she'd dropped in the garden, and it was clean. She picked it up with a smile and popped it on the kitchen worktop before skipping outside. It was still light but she was aware that she didn't have long before she'd have to get ready for bed. Step one of her plan was to leave the sausages and the note for the troll, she didn't know what step two was yet.

Looking around for signs of the troll, she crept down the garden. As she reached the riverbank she put down the sausages and slid the note beneath the plate so that it wouldn't blow away. With her arm outstretched, she sprayed the air freshener in anticipation of any nasty smells, and crept forward on to the bridge.

"Who's that stepping on MY bridge?" a voice roared. "I'll eat you up if you dare to cross!"

Dotti froze for a moment but, gathered her courage and edged forward.

"Who's that stepping on MY bridge?" the voice roared again. "I'll eat you up if you dare to cross!"

That's strange, she thought, *that sounds like a recording.* She stepped forward again, reaching the middle of the bridge.

"Who's that stepping on MY

bridge? I'll eat you up if you dare to cross!"

Something told Dotti that she needn't be scared. She knelt down on all fours and put her ear against the wood. She listened hard and could hear rustling coming from below. She took off her sunglasses and, spying a hole in the floor, peered through it with one eye.

She sprung back in surprise! Another eye! There was another eye staring right back at her.

Still on all fours, she moved as quietly as she could toward the edge of the bridge. She held her breath and, keeping her eyes tightly shut, leaned forward and peered underneath the bridge.

She counted to three and then opened her eyes. She found herself nose to nose with the troll!

"Ahhhhhhh!" they screamed together. Dotti jumped up as the troll scrambled back under the bridge.

"Ewww! Gross!" she squealed, throwing her hand over her nose. She peered back under the bridge, "That's *disgusting!*"

Embarrassed, the troll's cheeks turned a crimson red. "Sorry," he whispered, his voice shaky. "I trumps when I is scared!"

"Scared?" Dotti snapped. "Why

are *you* scared? It's me that should be scared. You're the one that eats children!"

"I, I don't!" he protested. "You eats trolls! All us trolls knows that peepkins eats us! This why we is hidin', so you can't smell our lovelies and cook us for munchin'."

Looking frightened, he retreated back under the bridge where he couldn't be seen. He could, however, still be heard:

'Sorry!" came the little voice from under the bridge. Dotti reached for the air freshener and squirted to mask the atrocious smell.

Standing up, as much to get away from the whiff as anything else, Dotti decided that it might be easier to talk if she sat on the riverbank where he could see her. Feeling brave she picked up the sunglasses and put them in her pocket, the troll wasn't *that* ugly. She pulled her trainers off and put them to one side.

She stepped off the bridge and

onto the soft mud, it squidged between her toes. Careful that she didn't slip, she sat down so that her legs dangled over the edge and her toes dipped in the water.

"Come out," she called "I promise not to eat you." The troll hesitated. "Come out, please," she tried again. "Just try not to trump, I'm not sure how much of this I can take!" she felt more confident now that she'd seen him for herself.

Out of the darkness two large eyes blinked at her. Raising his hand to shield his eyes from the light, the troll stepped out apprehensively. He was careful to stoop down so that he couldn't be seen from the kitchen window. The water swished around his shins as his feet moved gingerly across the pebbles under foot.

Dotti was taken by surprise. The description she'd heard of the smelly old troll wasn't particularly accurate!

For one he was no taller than her, his body was a little fluffy, rather than hairy, but it was brushed and tidy, and he had purple hair on his head.

He wore a pair of green shorts, which brought out the colour of his saucer-like eyes, and he had a large, wide mouth which hesitated between a frown and a smile. He blinked at Dotti.

5

"Hi," said Dotti, holding out her hand. "I'm Dotti, it's nice to meet you."

Puzzled, the troll also held out his hand, leaving it suspended in the air and said in a quiet, friendly voice, "I is Terence. Terence Trumpin'ton," feeling awkward he put his arm back at his side.

Dotti giggled, "That figures! You're supposed to shake hands, like this," she grabbed his hand. "It means we're friends."

"And you is not gonna' munch

me?" Terence asked uncertainly.

"I definitely won't munch, I mean *eat,* you," Dotti replied, giggling again. "You won't eat *me* will you?" she asked, suddenly remembering the warnings her mum had given her.

"Bleurgh!" said Terence. "Yuck! I is a vegemuncher, I don't munch no things tha's bin wrigglin' or breathin'!" the look on his face displayed the disgust he felt.

"Then I think we're going to get along just fine Terence Trumpin'ton," smiled Dotti.

"Dotti, Dotti! Where are you?" her mum called from the house. The sun had already set and it was starting to get dark. Terence shrunk back down into the water.

"That's my mum!" Dotti said, before calling back, "Coming Mum, I'm just in the tree!" she winked at Terence.

"OK, as long as you're not near that bridge young lady! Come on in now, it's getting dark."

Dotti didn't want to leave just yet but she knew that she'd better keep her mum on side otherwise she'd be banned from the garden all together! There was *so* much she wanted to learn about her new friend but she'd have to wait until tomorrow. She had one question that couldn't wait.

"Terence?" she asked.

"Yar?" Terence replied.

"Just tell me one thing. That voice you use for scaring people? How do you do that? It doesn't even sound like you!"

Terence put his hand in his pocket and pulled out a mobile phone!

He swiped the screen and pressed a button. *Who's that stepping on MY bridge? I'll eat you up if you dare to cross!'* It boomed.

"Is called TrollDub. Is a fancy-pancy App I 'as to use. Boss Troll says we trolls all be th' same. Scare you peepkins proper," he put the phone back in his pocket. "We trolls is clever, we be usin' sunshines an' make phones never run out," he winked, craftily.

Dotti couldn't quite believe her eyes or ears! For as long as she could remember, she'd been made to believe that trolls were nasty, stupid, dangerous creatures but from what she could see, that wasn't at all true! They'd even invented solar powered mobile phones!

"I'll be back tomorrow," she said as she got up to leave.

"Why?" Terence asked.

"Because we're friends, silly!"

Dotti smiled and blew Terence a kiss before running back up the garden, trainers in one hand, air freshener in the other.

6

The next day was Saturday and for once Dotti couldn't wait to get out of bed. She dressed at double speed and pelted down the stairs for breakfast. Dotti's mum was already out of bed and was shocked to see Dotti up so early. She looked at the clock.

"Dorothy Bell, I don't believe it! 9 AM on a weekend and you're out of bed! Are you OK?" she reached over and placed her palm on Dotti's forehead.

"Oh very funny, Mum," she pushed her mum's hand away dramatically and sat at the table. "I've got a project for school. I have to make a den in the garden and see how many bugs I can find."

Dotti's mum raised her eyebrows. "You're up early to do *homework?*" she quizzed. "Whatever next? Well, I suppose I shouldn't knock it."

She placed a plate of scrambled eggs in front of Dotti who tucked in, hungrily.

"Dotti? I meant to ask you last night. Who was that at the door yesterday?"

Dotti felt her face go pink. "Um, it was...a delivery man. Yeah, that's right, he, er, had the wrong house," she munched nervously. "Why? Were you expecting someone?" she cleverly deflected the question back at her mum, knowing exactly who she'd been expecting.

It was her mum's turn to blush with discomfort. "Oh! Er, no. No-one," she bluffed before picking up her mug of tea and heading back upstairs.

Perfect! Dotti thought to herself. With her mum out of the kitchen she could collect a few veggie snacks, for Terence without her mum watching her every move.

She opened the fridge and helped herself to carrots, potatoes and a cauliflower and crossed her fingers that none of them were on the menu for dinner tonight.

She reached under the sink for the air freshener again, although she had a feeling she might not need it so much today, put it in a bag with the food, a pen and a notepad, and made her way outside.

It was another beautiful day, perfect for making friends with a troll, Dotti considered. She hoped she wasn't too early.

She skipped through the damp

grass and as she approached the river, she could see Terence. There he was, hidden slightly behind a bush, washing himself with a bar of soap. He had a long branch with some straw tied to the end, bunched together to make a kind of scrubbing brush which he was using to wash his back.

Next to him, the sun caught the edge of a mirror which was hanging in the tree. Next to it was a twig from a willow tree, fashioned to act as a toothbrush and next to that was a pile of herbs that she assumed he used for toothpaste.

This troll really does worry about his appearance! Dotti thought self-consciously as she attempted to flatten down her uncontrollable curls.

She reached in the bag and held the air freshener out at arm's length.

"Morning!" She chirped.

Terence jumped a little,

"Oops! Sorry," he blushed and grabbed his shorts and put them on briskly, not wanting Dotti to see him in the nude!

Dotti squirted the air freshener and averted her gaze until he was decent. "Not a problem Terence, I came prepared," she smiled a cheery smile and pointed at the spray can. "I brought you a few things. I hope that's OK?" she felt a little shy now.

Terence sat down in the water and washed away the soap suds. Relaxing a little, he lay on his back and looked up at Dotti.

She be a funny Peepkin. He thought. *I 'ope she bubbled up this morn, I be told they smell funny.*

"No wrigglers in that sack be there?" he asked, not wanting to be tricked.

"No, it's vegetables. You like vegetables, don't you?" Dotti asked earnestly.

"I be likin' 'em best in th' dirt, but s'OK 'cos I can be rubbin' some in, add more yumness," he pushed himself up out of the water and waded over to the river bank. "Thankums, Peepkin," he said, sniffing Dotti's arm as she reached out and passed him the bag.

"Why are you sniffing me?" she asked.

"We trolls 'as bin told you peepkins is stinkers," Terence answered.

"HA!" exclaimed Dotti. "You can talk! You and your trumps! Peepkins, I mean, people don't smell unless they haven't had a wash in a long time and I have a bath every night. Mum makes me." She rolled her eyes.

"I tells yer, me can't help me trumps. Lucky it only be when me is nervy," he huffed. "Always bin trumpy, always will. But me keeps clean. Me bubbles up all the morns and swishes me gnashers," he pointed to his mouth. "Me eats mint leaves too, so me mowf-wind not stinkin'. See?" as he said this he huffed in Dotti's direction. She closed her eyes, Terence's breath made her hair blow back off of her face and she expected the stench to knock her backwards but it didn't and she was very pleasantly surprised.

"OK, sorry. I'll try not to scare you then, at least if I don't have my air freshener with me. Want to come and build a den with me? I told Mum that it was for homework, which it isn't, so if I don't build one she'll get suspicious."

"But 'er might look at me!" Terence looked concerned and nodded towards the kitchen.

"Hmm, I don't think she'll see you if we stay hidden in the bushes, but I've got an idea. Wait here."

Dotti quickly ran back to the house. When she returned she was holding a bundle of clothes.

"Here, try one of these T-Shirts on, they're a bit big for me at the moment. And if you wear my baseball cap, Mum will never know that you're not one of my friends!"

Terence held up the clothes and gave a nod of approval. He pulled on a green T-Shirt, to match his shorts of course, and a dark blue baseball cap. "Hansomes?" he asked.

Dotti giggled, "Very handsome. Now let's get started."

The early part of the day passed quickly. Dotti and Terence worked hard together to make a quite impressive den under the weeping willow tree at the bottom of the garden. The long, flowing, leafy branches that reached down to the grass were perfect for hiding behind.

Dotti found that making a den with a troll who permanently lived in her garden was very beneficial. He knew where to find the best branches, how to tie them together with reeds from the river so that they didn't slip and even how to fashion a kind of carpet out of twisted leaves.

She couldn't believe that Terence had been feared by the whole town. He was kind, gentle and helpful. All she had to do now was convince them that none of the rumours were true.

At lunchtime the two new friends sat inside their den and ate a picnic. As they relaxed, Dotti found out more about her new friend.

"So tell me more about trolls, Terence," she said.

"We trolls is all happy, we is nice. Long time afore, lotsa summers ago, us trolls lived happy in Troll Meadow.

Lots o' peepkins lived over t'other side o' th' big water. We is all happy. But when peepkin Mayor died, Papa Gruff took charge. Him's sons, thems Gruff brothers, be mean and horrid to all the peepkins *and* all we trolls.

Them Gruffs be greedy and take all niceness from Peepkins, so peepkins not be happy no more. Greedy Gruffs wanted Troll Meadow so they take woolly baas and moos from peepkins but say it be us trolls! peepkins be *sooo* angry."

He shook his head sadly as he remembered. "We trolls must protect us-selves so we guards th' wooden bridge crossing the big water. One day nasty Gruffs pretend they be fourleggers and tricks us and takes Troll Meadow.   We all be nervy and frightened so we all packs up and leave at moonshine," he let out a big sigh. "But poor Big Grampsy Troll.   He be guardin' us and he gets tricked by them Gruffs and we not see him again!" Dotti gasped.   "Now we's all livin' on our own. Me gets so lonelysome," Terence wiped a big, wet tear from his eye.

Dotti reached out and put her arm around her friend. She felt so sorry for him. Because of what the Gruff Brothers had done many years ago, the trolls were too frightened to live together and they were instructed to split up, taking any bridge they could find for shelter.

The Gruff Brothers had told the townsfolk that the trolls had been to blame for their sheep and cows going missing and made the people believe that the trolls were mean, nasty, smelly and grumpy, and would eat children for breakfast. They stole the trolls' land and because they didn't know where Grampsy was, the trolls became frightened.

They were afraid of people and decided that their best chance of protection was to live up to their reputation. If people thought they were scary, they would be left alone and they could live in peace.

Dotti knew what she had to do. She was very fond of her new friend and it just didn't make sense to her that people made their minds up without even meeting him. She was determined that everyone else should see what a nice troll he was too.

8

Dotti was excited. It was the first time she'd crossed the bridge and taken the short cut to school. Had she been less excited she may have taken advantage of the extra time in bed that she'd been so longing for! When her school friends called for her on their way, she grabbed her bag, kissed her mum goodbye and slammed the door behind her.

"Hi Dotti!" said Betsy.

"Hi!" chorused the group of friends.

Dotti smiled, "Come on, this

way..." she signalled towards her back gate.

"What? You're mad, we can't go that way!" exclaimed Toby.

"Actually...we can," Dotti put her hands on her hips and stood fast. "I've made friends with the troll." Toby gasped. Tilly laughed.

"No you haven't!" cried George.

Dotti raised her eyebrows. "How do *you* know?" she asked crossly.

"Because you can't be friends with a Troll, Dotti!" the children shrieked in unison.

"They *eat* children, Dotti! We won't even make it to school if we try and take the shortcut!" Betsy worried.

"Nonsense," Dotti said firmly.

"I'll see you at school, bet I get there first!" and she disappeared through her back gate leaving her friends to walk without her.

She made her way around the side of the cottage and ducked down as she passed the kitchen window. She ran across the grass, stopping at the bridge where Terence was brushing his teeth.

"Jolly morn, Dotti!" Terence muffled through a mouth full of herbs as he waved her across the bridge.

"Hey Terence!" She waved. Pulling her rucksack up on her back, she sprinted across the school field.

Dotti reached the playground with a full twenty minutes to spare. She found a warm spot in the sun and took out her reading book, secretly enjoying the peace and quiet. She opened her lunchbox and took out the apple she'd packed for break. She read for fifteen minutes and after a while she heard voices approaching her from behind.

"She's over there, look!" Betsy pointed. "Dotti, you're alive!" she screeched hugging her friend, dramatically.

Dotti laughed as she returned the hug. "And why do you think that is?" she asked.

"Perhaps she trapped the troll!" exclaimed George.

"Or she tricked him!" uttered Toby.

"Or, I was telling the truth," Dotti blurted out, shocked that her friends would suggest any different. "I *told* you, he's my friend."

Behind them, the headmaster rang the bell and called the children into class.

"Good morning children," greeted Miss Miller.

"Good morning Miss Miller, good morning everyone," the class chorused.

"What a lovely weekend it was. Would any of you like to share what you did?" she asked the class.

Dotti's hand shot up faster than lightning.

"Dotti!" Miss Miller was surprised, for Dotti wasn't normally one for contributing her thoughts so quickly. "How *lovely* of you to volunteer. What would you like to share?"

"Well, Miss Miller. You know that troll?" Dotti asked excitedly, pointing in the general direction of the river. Miss Miller shuffled uncomfortably in her chair. "The troll that lives under the bridge, at the end of my garden? At the end of the school field?" the class listened expectantly.

"Er, thank you Dotti, that's quite enough of that. Is there anyone else who would like to share this morning?" Miss Miller tried to ignore Dotti's insistence.

"HE'S MY FRIEND." Dotti shouted loudly, determined to be heard.

Miss Miller looked at her sternly. "That's quite enough young lady. We don't shout out in this class, as you well know and as for being friends with a troll? It's absolutely out of the question. He'd much rather eat you up!"

"Why would you want to be friends with a troll?" called a voice from the back of the class.

"He's got breath that smells like cow pats!" said Eve.

"Yeah and he smells worse than rotten eggs!" whispered Max.

"When he roars, it is so loud that your ears will pop!" exclaimed Monty.

"He's uglier than you could ever imagine," declared Lilah, "he's got big pointy ears and a big flat nose and yellow, rotting teeth."

"Actually, you're all wrong," proclaimed Dotti, a little upset. Why would no-one believe her? "He's none of those things. He brushes his teeth with herbs twice a day and he bathes in the river using soap. He has a very quiet voice and he isn't ugly, not to me anyway. He's actually quite sweet! He's even got a toadstool growing on his head."

She wanted desperately for her classmates to like him. "The *only* thing that isn't so nice is that he trumps," Dotti muttered, "but only when he's nervous!"

The children sniggered.

"Trumps?" questioned Miss Miller, "You mean..."

"Farts!" shouted a voice from the back of the room.

"Puffs!" sniggered another.

Giggles filled the air. Miss Miller blushed. "That's quite enough children! Now, tell me, why on earth would a stinky, child-eating troll be nervous?"

"Because he doesn't eat children and he's scared of peepkins...I mean, people. He's scared of people," Dotti spoke animatedly, her arms waving in the air.

"I think that's quite enough Dotti," Miss Miller stood up. "I will have no more talk about the troll. We do not wish to associate with that *ghastly* creature, and if it's becoming a problem then we must do something about it. Now, open your books and read in silence."

Miss Miller left and a murmur rippled across the room. The classroom assistant, Miss Heckford, shushed them gently as she put a sympathetic arm around Dotti's shoulders. Dotti felt deflated.   She thought that everyone would want to be friends with the troll too if they knew the truth about him!

The morning dragged and Dotti, feeling sad, found it hard to concentrate. It didn't help that her classmates would look over at her and then whisper amongst themselves. When lunchtime came, Dotti just wanted to eat her lunch in the playground alone.

She found herself an empty picnic bench underneath the oak tree overlooking the field and the river beyond. She opened her lunchbox and pulled out a sandwich.

"What does he eat then?" came a voice behind her. Dotti looked round to see Betsy standing next to her. She sat down next to Dotti. "Tell me, if he doesn't eat children, what *does* he eat?"

"He's a vegemuncher," Dotti mumbled quietly.

"A what?" asked Betsy.

"It means he's a vegetarian. He doesn't eat meat. He doesn't eat anything that moves, so of course he doesn't eat children?"

Betsy smiled. "And what does he look like?" she asked tucking into her lunch.

"He's about the same height as us, he's kind of fluffy, and blue, but he isn't scruffy. He has a mop of purple hair which he brushes every day and he has these two cute little yellow horns on the top of his head. He likes to look his best and even has a mirror hanging up in the tree so that he can check how he looks. He has a lovely smile, and dimples! I never knew trolls had dimples!"

Toby, George and Tilly came and joined the girls at the picnic bench. Dotti smiled at her friends before continuing. "He wears green shorts and I gave him a couple of T-shirts to wear so that my mum didn't get suspicious when we were playing in the garden."

"Playing in the garden?" Toby

scoffed.

"Yes," replied Dotti. "We were building a den and then we had a picnic and climbed some trees. He showed me how to hold a frog gently and tickle its tummy so that it croaks a song, and which plants along the riverbank are safe to eat."

Her friends couldn't believe what they were hearing. All of their lives they'd been told that the troll was nasty, horrid and dangerous, but here was their trusted friend telling them that he was the complete opposite. Their instinct told them that she was telling the truth.

All of a sudden Tilly piped up "Fine, you say he's friendly and nice, what about when he shouts at people when they try and cross the bridge?" she thought she'd caught Dotti out.

"TrollDub." Dotti replied assuredly before biting into a strawberry.

"TrollDub?" the children chorused.

"TrollDub! It's an App on his phone that all trolls have to use. The troll in charge, Boss Troll, says that they have a 'reputation' to live up to," she emphasised with her fingers, "and that they all *have* to sound scary. Trolls are actually very shy so they hide under their bridges and use TrollDub to scare people away," she explained.

George's eyes were wide. "He has

a phone? Which one?"

"Of course he does! He has to stay in touch with the other trolls somehow doesn't he?! It's some sort of smartphone or other," Dotti told the group. "It's *so* clever, it runs on solar power!" the gang were impressed.

"Why are they so shy?" Betsy asked.

"Because they're afraid that peepkins, that's what they call us, are going to eat them. Years ago the Gruff brothers ran them out of their own meadow where they'd been living happily for generations, you know the one where they're going to build the new houses? As time went by, rumours spread to the trolls that people were nasty and smelly and that we wanted to eat them."

"Hang on!" exclaimed Betsy, "That's what *we've* been told about *them*!"

"Exactly!" replied Dotti. "The Gruff brothers spread the rumours about the trolls so that they could steal their land. Most of the trolls escaped but Big Grampsy Troll wouldn't leave and the Gruffs caught him. A rumour spread amongst the trolls that the Gruffs had eaten him." The children gasped in unison.

"In order to protect the trolls, the respected Elder Trolls told them to spread out. They have to stay hidden and scare people away from the bridges where they live so that they don't get caught."

"Why on earth would we want to eat trolls?" asked Toby.

The children were agreeing with one another when something caught Dotti's eye. "Oh no!" she yelled. "Look,

over there," Dotti pointed to the van that had just pulled into the car park. "It's them!"

"The Gruff Brothers! Troll exterminators! Oh no!" yelled Betsy realising what was happening. "We *have* to stop them!"

"Miss Miller!" realised George, "She must have rung them when she left the classroom. What do we do?"

"Follow me!" shouted Dotti who was already sprinting towards the river. "I've already put them off the scent once but now we'll have to move Terence, keep him safe."

"How are we going to do that?" asked Tilly as they ran across the grass.

"I've got an idea, don't worry." Dotti called back to her. "Hurry!"

10

The children reached the bridge and as Dotti ran straight across, the others hesitated. "Come on!" she called "I've told you he won't hurt you. We *have* to help him!"

Her classmates looked at each other before bravely running across the bridge and into Dotti's garden. They took Terence by surprise and a putrid, eggy whiff filled the air.

"Oh no! We've scared him," Dotti realised. "Sorry guys. Terence, it's only me, are you there?" the children held their noses.

"Who's that stepping on MY bridge? I'll eat you up if you dare to cross!" Said a familiar voice.

"It's me Terence, put your phone away. Sorry we scared you but it's an emergency!" Dotti cried frantically. "Can you come out? Please!"

"Who them be?" Terence panicked, still hiding. "Why peepkins come?"

"Oh, they're my friends Terence, don't worry. I've told them all about you, they want to meet you!" urged Dotti.

Betsy stepped forward, still holding her nose. "Hello, Terence? We won't hurt you, but you need to come out because we think that someone else might."

Terence appeared cautiously from under the bridge, his eyes darting from left to right. The children were amazed. True to her word, in front of them stood a very clean, neat and tidy troll wearing green shorts and a blue T-Shirt. In one hand he held a half nibbled carrot and in the other, a mobile phone.

"Hellooo," he said quietly.

"Wow! A real life troll! Amazing!" Toby declared.

The children stared in wonder,

still holding their noses.   Terence noticed and reached back under the bridge reappearing with the can of air freshener Dotti had left with him. They all giggled as he sprayed it. Terence blushed.

Dotti looked serious. "Terence, there are some horrible people on their way down here. We need to hide you," she explained.

"Who be the 'orrids?" Terence asked with fear in his eyes, already knowing the answer.

"The Gruff brothers!"   Dotti replied.

"Urrrrggghhhh!"
"Seriously?"

"Spray, Terence, spray!" the group begged.

George, who had very wisely stayed to keep lookout on the bridge, called out to his friends "Quickly! They're on the way, and Miss Miller's with them!"

The children sprang into action. Dotti grabbed Terence's hand and pulled him into the den. Betsy found the hat he'd been wearing at the weekend and put it on his head. George grabbed a sheet from the washing line and laid it out on the grass. Tilly and Toby laid themselves on the sheet, as though sunbathing. George pretended he was bug hunting and Betsy and Dotti pretended they were doing a headstand competition.

Miss Miller and the three Gruff brothers appeared on the opposite side of the riverbank.

"How did you children get over there?" she demanded angrily. "You should be at school." The children stopped what they were doing and looked at their teacher, innocently.

"We walked, Miss," Dotti replied confidently. "It *is* lunchtime."

"How did you get there so quickly?" she questioned suspiciously, looking up and down the riverbank. "You *know* you aren't allowed to use the bridge."

"Where is he then?" interrupted the eldest Gruff brother, Bill. He was holding a large, troll-sized net.

"Let me at him," the middle-sized Gruff brother, Bobby, growled as he poked a long, sharp stick in the direction of the bridge.

The smallest brother, Benji, bustled behind them all with a large spray can of TROLL-KILLER in his hand. "I'll get him, let me through."

"Calm down Bobby, Benji. He'll be here somewhere," Bill stepped forward carefully onto the bridge, waving his net in the air. "Here trolly, trolly," he sing-songed. "We know you're here! We ain't gonna hurt ya!"

The den began to shake and a strong eggy smell filled the air. "Over there!" pointed Bobby.

"Enough of this," declared Benji impatiently as he pushed past, nudging the teacher as he did so.

"Wooahhhh!" Miss Miller screamed as she lost her balance. Her high heels were stuck in the mud on the riverbank and although she reached for some branches to steady herself, her hands slipped too.

The children watched as their teacher toppled forwards, her head was aimed at the water, and rocks beneath! Before anyone could stop him, Terence leapt into action. Bounding out from under the weeping willow he slipped down the muddy bank and towards Miss Miller.

"Get him!" the Gruff brothers shouted together and, without a second thought for the unfortunate teacher, all three pounced at him with their troll-catching weapons. Terence paid no attention to the danger he was in and in one swift movement dived into the river, toward certain danger!

It took a moment for Miss Miller to realise what had happened. Something soft and fluffy had cushioned her landing and prevented her from hitting her head. Her clothes were damp but she was unharmed. She breathed a sigh of relief, until she realised who'd saved her, and when she did, she let out a little screech.

She scrabbled to push herself up, unhooking Terence's arms which were still clasped around her middle. She turned to look at the troll, not sure what to expect. Terence lay on his

back with his eyes closed, he wasn't
moving.

"Terence!" Dotti shrieked in
alarm.

"Excellent!" Bill smiled and
rubbed his hands together. "You can
put that spray away Benji, this is gonna

be easier than we thought."

"Terence, no!" Dotti screamed and jumped into the shallow water, shoes and all.

The Gruff brothers waded in to the water with purpose, a wicked look in their eyes. Dotti stood in front of Terence and Miss Miller, guarding them.

"Move!" Bill stormed.

Dotti shook with fear. "If you want Terence, you'll have to get past me first!" she shouted, angry tears staining her cheeks.

"Stop this!" Miss Miller used her teacher voice and the Gruff brothers stood to attention. She stepped forward with authority. "You!" she pointed at Bill Gruff, "Get rid of that net. And you," she pointed at Bobby Gruff, "put that stick down. Now!" They obeyed without argument, dropping their weapons in the water. "And if you even *think* about spraying that can in this direction, young man, you'll have me to answer to." Benji Gruff backed away from his brothers and put his can on the riverbank.

Dotti took the opportunity to check on her friend. Kneeling in the water, she gently stroked Terence's cheek. She whispered in his ear. "Are you OK, Terence? Can you hear me?"

The friends waited on the bank, quiet as mice.

Terence opened his left eye and

whispered back, "Is they gone yet?"

Dotti whispered her reply "No, but Miss Miller has got them under control, don't worry, she's pretty good at that," she winked.

"Is it...he...OK?" Miss Miller enquired, sounding genuinely concerned.

"I think so, Miss," Dotti replied. "Although he might be a bit better if *they* weren't here!" she pointed at the Gruff brothers who watched, stony faced and motionless.

"Boys!" she spoke to the brothers, "Help Mr...Troll up, please."

Reluctantly they came over and helped Terence to his feet. "Now, off you go, we won't be needing your help anymore."

"But, Miss Miller, he's a nuisance, he's vermin. We must get rid of him!" Bill argued.

"I think you will find, Mr Gruff, that Mr Troll..."

"Terence." Dotti corrected.

"Sorry, Terence. I think you will find that Terence has just saved my life, whereas you," she pointed at the brothers, one at a time, "didn't consider anyone other than yourselves. You rushed to capture him, rather than help me!" she turned to Terence. "Thank you, Terence, for your selfless act. You chose to save me even though your life was in danger."

The Gruff brothers collected

their tools moodily and trudged away.
Terence blushed.

"What was that?" Miss Miller
wrinkled her nose.

"We *did* warn you!" chortled
George.

"He can't help it!" Dotti laughed.
"He does it when he's nervous or
embarrassed!"

"Ahem," Miss Miller coughed. "I
think lunch break is over, don't you?
Back to school children. Oh, and don't
forget to take the short route!"

She wafted the smell away and
ushered the children across the bridge
and back to school. She smiled her
appreciation at Terence as they left.

Terence hadn't expected anything more than a little acceptance following the afternoon's events but he was taken by surprise.

Miss Miller told the headmaster what had happened, who told the school secretary, who told a dinner lady, who told her husband, who was a journalist.

Mr Scoop had grabbed his notepad and paper and rushed to school and by afternoon break he was sat on the riverbank talking to Terence.

The troll explained the whole story to Mr Scoop, starting with Troll Meadow and how the Gruff brothers had forced the trolls away from their home and how they now earned a living catching trolls.

"That's awful, Terence, absolutely awful. I'm so sorry that we've been wrong about you this whole time!"

"Don't you be worryin'. I 'as bin 'appy, but lonelysome under me bridge," Terence answered.

"Well, I don't think you're going to be lonelysome, er I mean lonely, for much longer. May I take a quick picture?" Mr Scoop asked.

"Yar," Terence smiled widely.

The two were now firm friends and Mr Scoop was determined to clear Terence's name. After shaking hands, Mr Scoop hot-footed it back across the school field waving his goodbyes and shouting: "Deadline to catch! Watch out for tomorrow's paper!"

Terence wasn't really sure what Mr Scoop was talking about but he *was* sure about 3 things:

1. Mr Scoop definitely didn't want to eat him.

2. He hadn't trumped the whole time Mr Scoop had been there.

3. He wasn't going to be lonely any more.

The next day Terence waited for Dotti to get home from school. He watched her race all the way across the field and across the bridge waving something in the air.

"Look, Terence! You're famous!" she folded out the newspaper and held up the front page.

THE DAILY NEWS

Troll plays a trump card!

Yesterday our friendly neighbourhood Troll, Terence Trumpington, bravely saved the life of local teacher Miss Miller. When asked about the rumours of him being a child-eater he told us that he is in fact a vegetarian!

Terence read the headline. "Oooooh, look at that!" he exclaimed, blushing. Dotti held her nose. "Don't be worrying Dotti, no trumpsin' now." Dotti laughed.

"Dotti!" came her mum's voice from the house. "Is there something you need to tell me, young lady?" she asked as she ambled down the garden.

"I already told you, Mum. I made friends with the troll. Meet Terence," she held out her arm and introduced her friend.

"It seems that looking at this," she held up another copy of the newspaper. "I got you all wrong. I'm sorry Terence," she turned to Dotti, "and I think I also owe you an apology too, Dotti," Dotti looked surprised. "I know I said you couldn't make friends with a troll, but I was wrong. I'm a little cross that you ignored my instruction not to look for Terence, but I understand your reasons for doing it. You didn't listen to rumours and were brave enough to find out who he was for yourself."

Dotti thought about what her mum said then asked cheekily, "So I can go across the bridge to school now, can't I?"

Her mum laughed and rolled her eyes. "Yes, you can take the short cut to school. And you, Terence, are welcome to join us for dinner whenever you wish."

"Thankin' you, Mrs. I not be eatin' wrigglers, me belly only likes veggies. I 'ope that bes alright with yer?"

"I'm sure that can be arranged Terence, don't you worry."

"Brilliant!" Dotti exclaimed. She and Terence high-fived. "I can't wait for tomorrow. I get to see you, play in our den," she grinned at Terence, "**and** I get a lie in!"

"You is funny, Dotti!" Terence remarked. "Jus' you waits 'til I tells Boss Troll, he's not never gonna' b'lieve wot I tells him!"

"Well, I know just how to solve *that* Terence, where's your phone?" they posed for a picture. "Cheese!"

Dotti tittered. "He can't argue with a selfie now, can he?"

"I 'spose not!" Terence agreed.

"Dotti?"

"Yes, Terence?"

"I mus' be thankin' you."

"What for, Terence?"

"For bein' my friend."

Dotti grinned "You don't have to thank me Terence. All I wanted to do was prove that you weren't a horrible monster. And you're not. The stories never *actually* made any sense to me anyway. You might not *look* like everyone else but that doesn't matter. You're kind *and* gentle *and* thoughtful. The best thing is that you're my friend," Terence smiled the biggest smile he never thought was possible. "I can't wait to see what adventures we're going to have!"

What do you remember?

1. How many little birds can you find inside the book?

2. How old is Dotti?

3. What colour shorts does Terence wear?

4. How many Gruff brothers are there?

5. What does Terence like to eat?

6. What do Dotti and Terence build in the garden?

7. What is Dotti's teacher's name?

8. What three things do the Gruff brothers use to try and catch Terence?

9. What is the name of Mr Scoop's newspaper?

10. What are Dotti and Terence looking forward to now that they are friends?

 Classroom Questions

1. Why didn't Dotti believe the rumours about Terence being a child-eating troll? Do you think she was right for trying to make friends with him?

2. Terence has been living on his own for a long time, how do you think he has been feeling?

3. Who do you think was more scared when they first met? Terence or Dotti? Why?

4. Even though Dotti was very keen to tell Miss Miller about Terence, she normally doesn't put her hand up in class. Why do you think that might be?

5. Can you explain how you think Dotti showed courage?

6. How do you think Dotti felt when her friends didn't believe her?

7. Why do you think Terence saved Miss Miller?

8. In what way do you think things will change for Terence now that everyone knows he is kind?

About the Author

Caroline graduated from London Metropolitan University in Modern History and worked in Marketing before having a family and focussing on supporting children in both Primary and Secondary Education. She now lives with her husband, children, two cats, guinea pig and hamster in Hampshire.

Caroline is also an Ambassador for a charity called The Courage Foundation UK who raise money to support bereaved children and their families.

You can find out more about the wonderful work they do at: **www.thecouragefoundation.uk**

Printed in Poland
by Amazon Fulfillment
Poland Sp. z o.o., Wrocław